STEP BY STEP

Down
in the Shed

Diane Wilmer
illustrated by Nicola Smee

Aladdin Books
MACMILLAN PUBLISHING COMPANY
NEW YORK

When Nicky woke up, it was
raining hard. So he spent
the morning in his room,
drawing and cutting out.
Jenny stayed with him, curled
up on an old sweater.

It was quiet and peaceful
until Mom rushed in.

"Do you have anything for the school rummage sale?" she asked.
Nicky found a truck and some toy soldiers.
"You can have these," he said.
"What about that old sweater?" said Mom.
"It's got a big hole in it," said Nicky.
But Mom lifted Jenny off her cozy bed and put the sweater into her bag.

Jenny was very, very angry.
She hissed and stalked off.
"Mom," said Nicky.
"Jenny likes that sweater."

But Mom didn't hear.
"I'll take this bag over
to the school right now,"
she said.

But it was too wet outside.
"Oh well,"
she said.
"I'll have to take it later."

She left the bag in the hall,
but it kept falling over.
So she put it in the kitchen
where it got in everybody's way.

"I'll take it out to the shed,"
said Dad.

It was quiet and dry inside the shed. "We'll leave it here till it stops raining," he said.

But it rained all day.

It wasn't until bedtime that Nicky
missed Jenny.
"Where is she?" he asked.
Nobody knew.

He and Claire looked all over the house.

Under the stairs.

In the cupboards.

Under the bed.   Behind the couch.

They couldn't find Jenny anywhere.

Mom went out into the backyard.
"Here, kitty kitty kitty," she called.
But Jenny didn't come.

"Maybe she's found a new friend," said Dad.
"I'm sure she'll turn up in the morning."

In the morning, as soon as Nicky woke up, he ran downstairs and open the back door.

"Here, Jenny! Here, kitty!" he called.

But still she didn't come.

Nicky began to cry.
He didn't want his breakfast.
He didn't even want to play with Dan.

"I just want Jenny," he sobbed.

Dad tried to cheer him up.
"Look, it's stopped raining,"
he said.
"Let's take the bag over
to the school."
"Okay," said Nicky.

It was quiet and dry inside the shed.
Dad picked up the bag and something
jumped out.
"JENNY!" cried Nicky.

"So *that's* where you've been,"
said Dad.
"She likes this sweater a lot,"
said Nicky. "I'm going to keep it
for her."
"Good idea," said Dad.
"Keep it for her rainy
day naps."